RICHARD SCARRY'S
The Cat Family
Takes a Trip

A GOLDEN BOOK • NEW YORK

Western Publishing Company, Inc., Racine, Wisconsin 53404

Discard

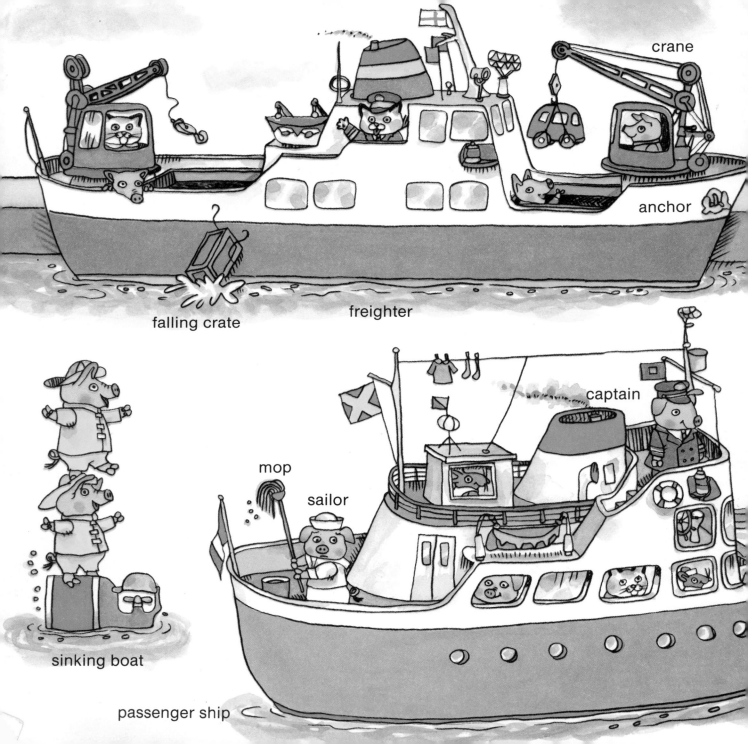

crane

anchor

falling crate

freighter

mop

sailor

captain

sinking boat

passenger ship

lighthouse

sailboat

The Cat family is on the way to the railway station to pick up Big Hilda Hippo, who is coming to visit them. On the way, they pass the busy harbor full of boats.

laundry

power barge

tugboat

life preserver

Cat family

It is a very busy day in the busy harbor. Lots of things are happening.

fire fighter

fireboat

collision

police boat

submarine

buoy

raft

fire

towline

tugboat

fishing boat

fishermen

flag

patrol boat

ferryboat

tower

HOTEL

POST OFFICE

postman

tree

The Cat family drives through Busytown, where everybody is very busy.

chimneys

windows

artist

café

reporter

Mr. Frumble

office building

THE NEWS

ABC

flagpole

There are many different
stores in Busytown.
Can you see them all?

HARDWARE

FLORIST

BARBER

drummer

flowerpot

bulldozer

small pickle car

fish truck

chimney sweep

weather vane

neighbor

baby carriage

mouse car

ICE CREAM

GROCERIES

ladder

bicyclist

Cat family

tuba player

pencil car

sign

Meter Maid Millie

Never park your car on a roof, because Meter Maid Millie gives parking tickets.

roof

CLOCKS

SHOE REPAIR

Eyeglasses

fire hydra

pickles

motorcycle

TV antenna

pencil car

fountain pen

traffic light

TV REPAIR

BOOKSTORE

crosswalk

BANK

LIBF

clock

police officer

photographer

Here is Main Street.
Look! Mr. Frumble
has lost his hat.

bug car

bug taxi

TAXI

street
cleaner

broom

grandmother

tricycle

baby

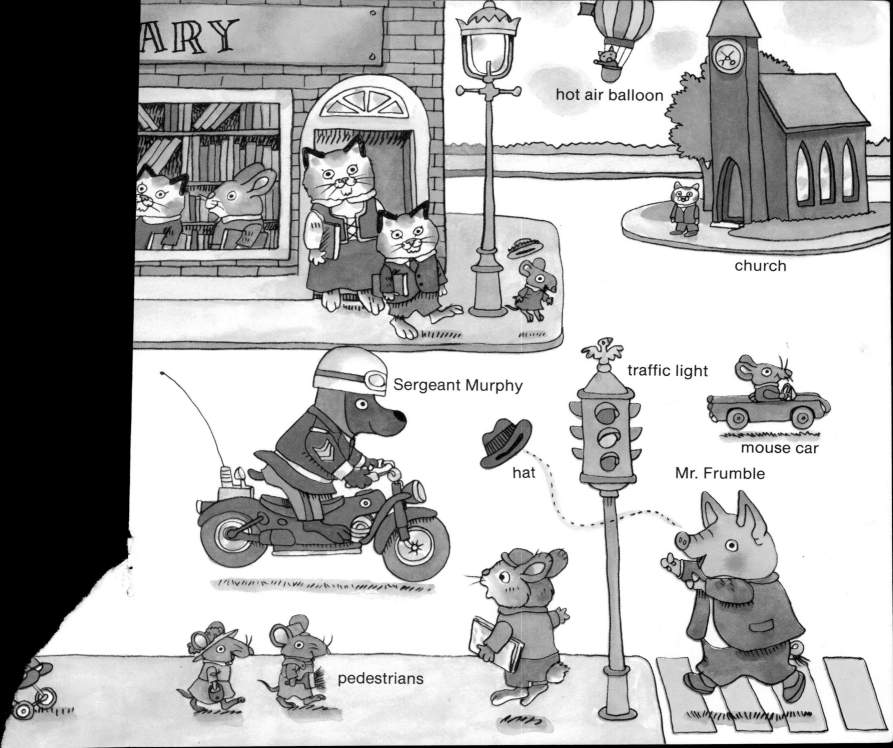

hot air balloon

church

Sergeant Murphy

traffic light

mouse car

hat

Mr. Frumble

pedestrians

pilot

airplane

brown

white

black

green

blue

orange

violet

yellow

red

teakettle

eggs

bread

slice

eggbeater

frying pan

juice

grater

stove

saucepan

knife

sponge

toast

spatula

strainer

colander

butter

toaster

father

baby

Many people live outside of town.
Big Hilda Hippo's train has not arrived yet,
so the Cat family decides to take
a ride in the country.

sun

The Cat family drives by the
Pig family's house.
The house is full
of things.

artist

picture

pen

paint box

pencil

brush

sweater

jacket

pants

overalls

dress

blouse

skirt

rain hat

hat

cap

hat

scarf

handbag

belt

raincoat

purse

shoes

boots

sneakers

umbrella

toothbrush

cabinet

towel

sink

toilet

bathtub

pencil car

helicopter

tree

tree house

hat

snowsuit

coat

bathrobe

pajamas

bell

balcony

Would you like
to live in a tree house?

Cat family

door

door
handle

mother bug

baby bug

corn

tractor

small bug tractor

corncrib

roof

They come to a farm.
On the farm, farmers
grow many things
for us to eat.
Do you like corn?

paint

windows

porch

door

pump

ax

wood

scarecrow

weather vane

windmill

barn

poster

rope

ladder

saw

truck

rooster

chick

hen

Back in town again, there is some trouble. Oh, dear! Mr. Frumble has hit a fire hydrant, the cherry picker has hit a street light, and the garbage truck has scattered paper everywhere.

Cat family

street cleaner

cherry picker

Mr. Frumble

street sweeper

tow truck

garbage truck

gas station
attendant

gas pump

TICKETS

clock

NEWSSTAND

thermometer

ticket window

Big Hilda Hippo

magazines

stationmaster

dining car

cook

passengers

BAGGAGE

Finally they arrive at the railway station. Big Hilda Hippo has just gotten off the train. They are all so happy to see her.

baggage room

engineer

steam engine

mechanic

tracks

Mother Cat has prepared a lovely meal for Big Hilda Hippo.

Mother Cat

food

fork

salt and pepper

glass

plate

knife

napkin

chair